GOSCINNY AND UDERZO
PRESENT
AN ASTERIX ADVENTURE

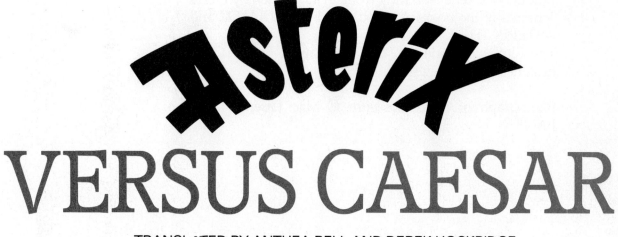

Asterix
VERSUS CAESAR

TRANSLATED BY ANTHEA BELL AND DEREK HOCKRIDGE

HODDER AND STOUGHTON
LONDON   SYDNEY   AUCKLAND

This book is based on the film ASTERIX VERSUS CAESAR, a co-production by Gaumont, Dargaud and Les Productions René Goscinny, from an adaptation by Pierre Tchernia of the books ASTERIX THE GLADIATOR and ASTERIX THE LEGIONARY.
The film was made by Paul and Gaëtan Brizzi. Chief designer: Michel Guérin.

Photograph of the Colosseum © Mac Laren/IMAGE BANK

British Library Cataloguing in Publication Data

Asterix versus Caesar: the book of the film.
  I. Bell, Anthea   II. Hockridge, Derek
  III. Goscinny   IV. Uderzo
  V. Asterix et la surprise de Cesar. *English*
  843'.914[J]   PZ7

  ISBN 0-340-39722-5
  ISBN 0-340-39723-3 (pbk)

Original edition © **Les Editions Albert René, Goscinny-Uderzo, 1985**
English translation © Les Editions Albert René, Goscinny-Uderzo, 1986
Exclusive licensee: Hodder and Stoughton Ltd
Translators: Anthea Bell and Derek Hockridge

First published in Great Britain 1986 (cased)

First published in Great Britain 1988 (limp)
This impression 93 94 95 96

Published by Hodder Dargaud Ltd,
Mill Road, Dunton Green, Sevenoaks, Kent TN13 2YA

Printed in Belgium by Proost International Book Production

The year is 50 BC. Gaul is entirely occupied by the Romans. Well, not entirely . . . One small village of indomitable Gauls still holds out against the invaders. And life is not easy for the Roman legionaries who garrison the fortified camps of Totorum, Aquarium, Laudanum and Compendium . . .

63

1008
011

FLESH 2

152
010
511
261

205

SOLES 273

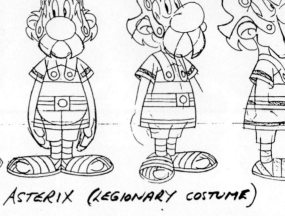

ASTERIX (LEGIONARY COSTUME)

ROMAN SWORD

I'm Asterix, the hero of this adventure. Those crazy Romans thought they'd have another go at our little Gaulish village, and the whole thing ended up in Rome, with splendid celebrations organized by Caesar in our honour. You're about to hear how Obelix and Dogmatix and I took the opportunity to give our old friend Julius a nice surprise.

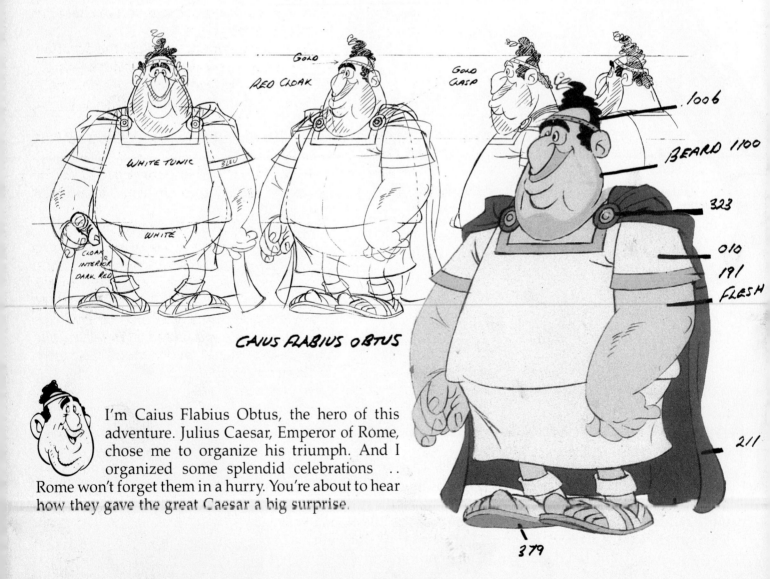

GOLD

RED CLOAK

WHITE TUNIC   BLEU

WHITE

CLOAK INTERIOR DARK RED

GOLD CLASP

1006

BEARD 1100

323

010
191
FLESH

211

CAIUS FLABIUS OBTUS

I'm Caius Flabius Obtus, the hero of this adventure. Julius Caesar, Emperor of Rome, chose me to organize his triumph. And I organized some splendid celebrations .. Rome won't forget them in a hurry. You're about to hear how they gave the great Caesar a big surprise.

379

It was a lovely day. All was peace and gladness in our little Gaulish village. The fortified Roman camp of Totorum, on the other hand, was nothing like as peaceful … apparently a keen new decurion had just arrived, and he was giving the centurion a tough time. Geriatrix happened to overhear them when he was out picking mushrooms in the forest.

'All well, sentry?' this centurion was asking anxiously. He was a nervous sort of character. 'Nothing stirring?'

'All well, centurion, sir!' said the decurion, who was on sentry duty. 'Nothing stirring!'

'They're lying low, then. Thank Jupiter!'

Here the new decurion went right off his chump.

'Yes, thank Jupiter! Now's our chance! Let's lay them low! Let's crush 'em!'

'Hold on just one moment, Decurion Incautius,' said the centurion. 'You're new here, right?'

'Arrived with the last cohort, sir!'

'A word in your ear, decurion: don't you ever go attacking those indomitable Gauls! This is the most dangerous village in the whole of Gaul. And of all its inhabitants, the two worst are a great big bloodthirsty brute with savage ferocity written all over him, and a tiny but terrifying warrior, a total stranger to all proper human feeling.'

By Toutatis, the Romans weren't the only ones to fear us, and with good reason! The wild boars in the forest had better look out if they wanted to save their bacon, because Obelix and I were going hunting.

On our way, we met a girl walking down the village street. And that was how the story really began. Obelix was struck all of a heap. He bumped into a tree. The tree was struck all of a heap too.

'Enjoying yourself, Obelix, pushing trees over while I'm up them cutting mistletoe?' inquired our druid Getafix, emerging rather suddenly from the foliage.

'Trees?' said Obelix. 'What trees?'

'These trees!'

'Oh, you mean this tree! Well . . . er . . . it's an untidy sort of forest, anyway. Trees all over the place!'

And picking up the tree, Obelix replanted it, druid and all.

Then he did a very odd thing. He started off back towards the village. I grabbed his breeches to hold him back.

'You're going the wrong way for the boars!'

'Am I? All right, let's get a move on.'

So we got a move on. A few boars tried moving on too, but we soon caught up with them and invited them home for dinner . . .

9

Nothing like a good roast to put some beef into you ... or brawn, if it's Obelix eating wild boar.

'Good boar, Obelix?' I said.

'Yes ... yes, but somehow I don't feel very hungry any more ...'

By Toutatis, this was really serious! I went to call the druid.

'O druid Getafix!'

'Yes?' said Getafix.

'I'm worried ... Obelix isn't well. He'd only just begun on a boar when he said he didn't feel hungry.'

'Hm ... did he have anything else first?'

'Only two boars.'

'Two boars ... that hardly counts. I'd better take a look at him!'

On our way back to my house we saw that golden-haired Gaulish rose again.

'By the way, Getafix,' I asked, 'who is she?'

'She's ... hullo, hullo, here comes the invalid!'

'What?'

'Oh, yes,' said Getafix, 'I can see he's lost his appetite all right! Ho, ho!'

Sure enough, there was Obelix, wandering down the road after the pretty girl like a man in a daze.

'Where are you going, Obelix?'

'To deliver a large menhir.'

'But you haven't got any menhirs on you!'

'I haven't?' said Obelix. 'Why, so I haven't!'

Poor old Obelix! Even Dogmatix was giving him a funny look.

Getafix introduced us. 'This is Panacea, the chief's niece, just back from studying in Lutetia. Panacea, have you met Asterix?'

'Hullo, Panacea!' I said. 'Why, how you've changed! When you left for Lutetia you were still a little girl with your hair in pigtails, like Obelix. You remember Obelix?'

'Yes, of course! The one who fell into the potion when he was a baby! How are you, Obelix?'

'F . . . f . . . fine, P-p-p-anacea . . .'

But Panacea was on her way.

Getafix fell about laughing. 'Ho, ho, ho! Hee, hee, hee! Obelix, my dear fellow, you're in love, that's what it is! Sorry, but I don't have any magic potions to cure you of that!'

And the druid went back to his cauldrons, leaving Obelix looking stunned. Well, Panacea was stunning all right. I felt sorry for him.

'Between you and me, Obelix, you like little Panacea, don't you?'

All the reply I got was a kind of a mumble.

'You like her *that* much?'

The mumble came out a bit louder.

'Then why not give her a present?'

'That's a good idea!' said Obelix.

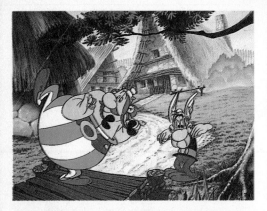  

No sooner said than done: a stoutish streak of blue and white lightning shot across the little bridge where we were standing, and came back carrying a large present tied up with a big bow.

'You're never going to give her that?' I gasped.

'Why not? It's my very best menhir!'

'But ... but you want to give her ... well, say, flowers! Go and pick her a nice bunch of flowers in the forest. She'd like that!'

'I suppose you know best, Asterix ...'

And next thing I knew, Obelix was back clutching a little bunch of flowers to match the stripes on his trousers.

'A very nice bouquet,' I said encouragingly. 'Very poetic. Go on, call her!'

'Ooh, no, I wouldn't dare! You do it!'

'Anything you say ... PANACEA!'

'Ssh! She might hear you!'

'Panacea,' I said, 'my friend Obelix has a present for you.'

Obelix stuck out his arm, with the flowers on the end of it.

Not wishing to disturb their billing and cooing, I was about to steal away, when suddenly ...

13

 Events took a sensational turn! Panacea threw her flowers in the air and rushed into the arms of a handsome young man, and I don't mean Obelix.

Lost in his blissful dreams, Obelix didn't immediately notice that Panacea was already miles away. Then he did.

Chief Vitalstatistix came along and shattered his last illusions, if any. 'That,' he said, 'is Tragicomix, son of Chief Dramatix. They're engaged. Sorry, but you don't stand a chance!'

Obelix burst into floods of tears.

'You whet my interest,' said the chief. 'Dry up! What's the matter?'

'He's in love,' I explained.

Meanwhile the young couple were wandering off into the forest, unaware that a four-footed friend was following them, keeping its distance . . .

I'd never seen Obelix in such a state before! I did my best to cheer him up. Then Dogmatix suddenly came racing back to us, with a pink ribbon in his mouth. Panacea's ribbon! By Belenos . . . what had happened?

'Where did you find it, Dogmatix?' I asked.

The faithful hound led us off to the forest as fast as he could go. All of a sudden he stopped beside a bush.

'Obelix, Dogmatix has found something!'

'Found what?'

'A helmet! The Romans were here! They must have kidnapped Panacea and Tragicomix!'

Obelix cheered up no end at the prospect of a fight.

'Goody, goody, goody! Let's go!'

'No, Obelix! It wouldn't be fair to keep the Romans to ourselves. We must go back to the village and tell the others.'

 And we went into the usual routine. Cauldron. Hot water. Secret ingredients added one by one in the darkness of Getafix's house. The potion started bubbling merrily, and then fiercely. The lobster went in. A strange and penetrating aroma rose to our nostrils.

We queued outside the druid's door, keeping in line like the good Gauls we are, in spite of the also-routine grumbles of 'Stop pushing at the back there!'

Geriatrix, the oldest inhabitant, was privileged to have first taste of the magic potion which gives us superhuman strength.

And for once, just for once, Obelix wasn't agitating to have some too.

'Notice anything, Getafix? I'm not asking for any magic potion today, am I? You want to know why? Because I jolly well know that if I do go asking for a taste of your magic potion you'll just say I fell-into-the-cauldron-as-a-baby-and-rhubarb-rhubarb-gnagnagnagna . . . that's why!'

At last the signal was given:
'CHARGE, BY TOUTATIS!'

  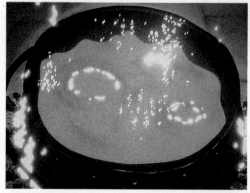

So terrible a battle ensued that, out of consideration for my more sensitive readers, I will pass over it in silence. Silence fell on the fortified Roman camp too.

Over by the camp fence, I saw Centurion Terminus, up against it but still with some fight left in him.

'Veni, vidi, non vici,' he admitted. 'Oh, well, what's brave, what's noble, let's do it after the high Roman fashion, and how can man die better than facing fearful odds, for the ashes of his fathers and the temples of his Gods . . .'

'Never mind the poetry,' I said, 'just tell me where the prisoners are, or do you want me to thump you?'

'Er . . . um . . . no. Well, about those prisoners. What a mix-up! If that idiot decurion, Incautius, hadn't tried to do his bit for Rome by arresting them, we'd all still be quietly growing lettuces. I . . . er . . . disposed of the prisoners, Gaul. They're on their way to Condatum* to join the Foreign Legion.'

I knew what had to be done.

'Hey, Obelix!'

'Just coming. Let me finish off one last Roman.'

'They *are* finished. And we're off to Condatum!'

*Rennes

On reaching Condatum, we thought we'd better ask a legionary the way to his headquarters. A patrol happened to be marching along right in front of us, feet pounding the road with measured tread.

'Shall we stop this patrol, Obelix?'

Ever ready to do his bit, Obelix waded in, fist pounding the Romans with measured punch. Obelix's bit was a bit much! I flipped my helmet! 'Look, we only needed to stop them!'

'Well, we did stop them!'

'There are times,' I said, 'when it pays to be polite, Obelix!' And grabbing a foot which was sticking out of the heap of Romans, I shook it briskly. 'Would you be kind enough to tell me the way to the Foreign Legion's barracks, please?'

'Third on the left and please stop hitting me.'

'Thanks. Ave.'

I decided to go in on my own. You never can tell, with Obelix ... his company manners occasionally leave something to be desired.

I introduced myself politely to the legionary on sentry duty.

'No entry!' he said. 'If you want to join up, Gaul, get in line like everyone else!'

'Listen, I only wanted some information ...'

'Get in line, I said!' he shouted.

Rather uncivil, I thought, for a military man. I had to make my point more forcefully. The sentry was much struck, but Obelix appeared rather puzzled.

'I don't honestly see the difference between Asterix's politeness and my politeness,' he muttered.

A little notice on a door said ENQUIRIES. I thumped on the door. Somebody spoke up inside.

'What is it? No one ever comes in here!'

I thumped harder. BOING!

'That's right, go ahead, break the door down!'

So I did. CRAASH.

'I'm enquiring,' I said politely, 'for a legionary called Tragicomix, pressed into the Foreign Legion in Armorica.'

'That sort of information's classified.'

I thumped again, harder. Not on the door this time.

'Stop it! Don't! Here's his travel warrant!'

I looked at it. This was serious! I called Obelix, but he seemed to be busy with a few little administrative formalities of his own.

'Asterix,' said Obelix, 'that Roman you were being very polite to is being very polite to me now. Can I be very polite back to him?'

'Carry on.'

'Chin up a bit, please, Roman . . .'

And the Roman legionary received another stunning display of Gaulish courtesy.

I told Obelix what I'd found out. 'Tragicomix and Panacea are bound for Africa! The only way to get there is to join the Roman army ourselves, and fast!'

So we went back and queued up with the other volunteers to join the Legion.

'This will send me into a decline,' said the sentry, who had only just finished falling.

After a while a Roman soldier came to help us enlist.

'Ah, there you are, my dear young fellows! Volunteers to join the Legion! Come right along in! I'm your good friend Decurion Dubius Status. If you'd be so very kind as to step this way ... now then, let's carve down your names. You, Briton – what are you called?'

'Paytoomuchtax, I say, what!'

'Don't we all? Next!'

'Peccadillo el Bonafidez, olé!'

'How do you spell it?' asked Dubius Status.

'Listen, decurion, never mind that,' I told him. 'Just carve down Olé! And we're Asterix and Obelix, so hurry up and carve us down too. We've got no time to waste!'

After these little formalities, the Roman army set about rigging its new recruits out as legionaries.

'Are we in the army now?' asked Obelix, rather surprised by his altered appearance. But the decurion wasn't so jovial any more.

'SILENCE!' he shouted. 'YOU'RE IN THE ARMY NOW!'

'Thanks,' said Obelix. 'That's what I wanted to know.'

'GET IN LINE!' shouted Decurion Dubius Status, coming over all excited. 'AND JUMP TO IT! We will now do a little drill.'

He was wasting his breath.

'You want me to be polite to him, Asterix?' asked Obelix.

'Not just yet, Obelix.'

'SILENCE, YOU TWO!' yelled the decurion, his temper fraying.

Unfortunately, there was a bit of a mis-understanding.

'What was that he said, old chap, what?'

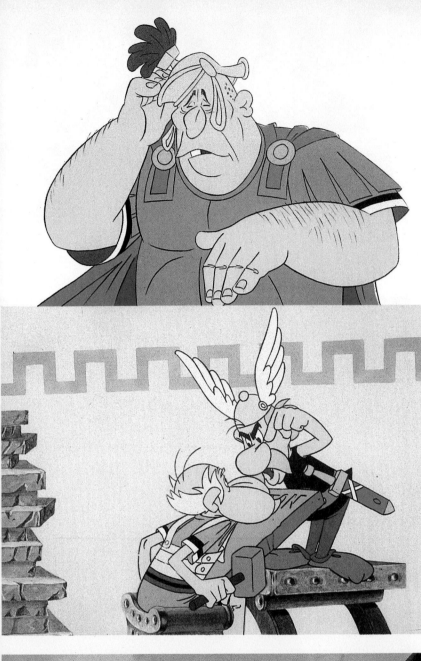

asked the Briton, in Ancient British.

'What's that Briton saying?' asked the decurion suspiciously.

But it still hadn't got through.

'Come again, old boy, what?' asked the Briton. 'Wot *you* what's up, what?' he asked us.

'What is that Briton getting at?' inquired the decurion again.

The Viking came to his aid.

'I think he ... what you say? ... he want to know what you say.'

'SILENCE!' yelled Dubius Status, by way of explanation.

Obelix shoved his own oar in too. 'SIIILENCE!'

I was getting quite worked up myself. 'Look, Roman, is this going on much longer? How about that drill? I'm in a hurry, you know.'

At that moment trumpets sounded somewhere in the barracks. The Spaniard, the Briton, the Goth and the Viking all perked up at once.

'ZUPPA! SOUP! 𝕾𝖚𝖕𝖕𝖊! SØUPE!'

I realized that I felt a little empty myself. So I followed the others to the mess.

Behind us, Dubius Status burst into tears. I had no idea why, but Obelix, who is not as dim as he may look, knew.

'Between you and me, Asterix, I think he's in love.'

And being cured himself must have reminded him of bacon and where it comes from, because he asked, 'I say, do you think they have boar here?'

'I wouldn't get too hopeful,' I said. 'The stronger the army, the worse its food! That's what keeps the men in a nasty fighting temper!'

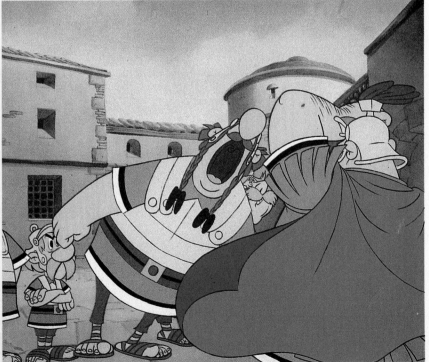

 It wasn't long before we knew the answer to Obelix's question: a legionary came in with a steaming cauldron. Ladle in hand, he filled our bowls – SPLOTCH! The mixture duly took effect on the Roman soldiers' temper.

'Yuk! I didn't know the Roman army was quite that strong!' I said. 'Er . . . joking apart, legionary, what *is* it?'

'Staple military rations . . . corn, bacon and cheese, all cooked up together to save time!'

'Is it like this every day?'

'No, you get double rations on Sundays!'

'You'd have to be a Briton to like this stuff!'

'Rather!' said the Briton happily. 'Scrumptious! Really super, don't you know, what!'

But Obelix wasn't taking any insults to what was closest to his heart, namely, his stomach. The two of us went to have a word with the cook.

'Hey! Do you do the cooking around here?'

'Yes,' he said. 'Why?'

'Because you're a rotten cook, that's why!'

Surprisingly, the cook didn't seem to take offence.

'Couple of gourmets we've got here, have we?' he asked sweetly. 'I suppose you'd like some fancy cooking? Want to give your orders?'

'Yes, please,' said Obelix. 'Wild boar.'

The cook's tone became sweeter than ever. 'Fancy cakes too? I bet you like fancy cakes!'

But then he changed his tune.

'YOU GET OUT OF MY KITCHEN, OR I'LL HAVE YOU IN THE COOLER!'

'I say, Asterix,' said Obelix, not to be outdone, 'can I be polite to him?'

'Go right ahead, my dear Obelix!'

So Obelix most politely gave him the chop, with a slug of something strong to help it down – and him, too – and dumped him in his own cauldron, punch-drunk.

When the cook had simmered down a bit, I said, 'Now, Roman, listen to me! Any time we're not satisfied with our food, we'll be paying you another visit!'

And we turned and marched out, leaving the cook in a terrible stew.

After lunch, we got down to business with Decurion Dubius Status, our instructor.

'Now then!' he told us. 'You're assigned to the Ist Legion, IIIrd Cohort, IInd Maniple, Ist Century. You have to repeat that lot when presenting yourself to a superior officer! You, little titch! Present yourself!'

'Right,' I said. 'Asterix the Gaul!'

'And I'm Obelix,' said Obelix, offering to shake hands, 'so what's your own name, then?'

'Decurion Dubius Status, Ist Legion, IIIrd Cohor . . . Grrr! Get back into line, will you? We're going to do some drill! Here's a pilum, Legionary Obelix. You have to try to hit that target the other side of the square. Off you go.'

Obelix's pilum sailed through the air with the greatest of ease, passed right through the target and in at the cookhouse door . . . homing in on the plumpest part of the cook's anatomy. He didn't seem to like it much.

'Here, just give me time to cook your boars, can't you?'

Somewhat surprised, Dubius Status decided to instruct us in the use of another weapon.

'We'll all do gladius drill! These are only pretend swords, of course, made of wood . . . come on, you! I'm attacking you. Defend yourself!'

Obelix did as he was told. Dubius Status too went sailing through the air in the direction of the cookhouse. The cook hadn't expected this extra ingredient.

'The soup's going to taste pretty funny at this rate, decurion!' he grumbled.

Commanded by Decurion Dubius Status, who decided we had done more than enough drill, we men of the Ist Legion, IIIrd Cohort, IInd Manithingummy, Ist Centiwhatsit left Condatum for the port of Massilia*, where we were to embark for Africa.

The decurion did a lot of shouting, at first. 'You bunch of barbarians! Less fooling around now, eh? Dragging our feet now, are we? Step out, then! For the greater glory of Rome! Quick march!'

Not a bad idea ... only rather than marching, we started running as fast as we could, in order to reach Massilia as soon as possible. We were feeling cheerful. But Dubius Status wasn't as keen as before, not at this pace.

'Halt! Brake for a break!'

We just laughed. 'Give us a break, decurion! We like running!'

Our column, though still on the move, had undergone a slight modification as to marching order.

Right at the back, our leader Dubius Status was speaking of leaving the Legion and returning to Rome to put his talents to use in some other line of business ...

At last we reached Massilia. The ship's captain seemed anxious to sail ... but not as anxious as we were.

'We're in a hurry! Gangplank up! Let go aft!'

'Wh ... what d'you mean, let go aft?'

Too late! We had cast off, the anchor chain was slowly rising, the mainsail was swelling in the breeze, and we were on our way ...

Dubius Status wasn't coming with us ... well, he'd have been all at sea, by Belenos!

*Marseilles

31

A few days' peaceful voyage brought us to the gates of a Roman camp.

Inside, of course, the place was full of Romans. I warned Obelix off them, just in case. 'Don't touch! They're friends of ours for now!'

'You mean we're friends with our enemies? I wish you'd explain, Asterix!'

But I thought this was a case of live now, philosophise later, so I took him off to the mess, where the man in charge was holding forth.

'The desert, ah, the desert ... wind, sand, sand and wind ... you'd be crazy to go out in this wind,' said the Roman in the mess. 'They must be in an even worse mess by now!'

I pricked up my ears. 'They? Who!'

'A couple of Gauls, a man and a woman.'

And he explained that Centurion Garulus Rumpus had taken a fancy to the woman (yes, that was Panacea all right), and he got rather fresh with her, which she did not appreciate, so then the other Gaul (Tragicomix, obviously!) stepped in, took the girl away in a stolen chariot, and the pair of them drove off into the desert, little knowing what it was like.

I could see there was no point in hanging around there any longer, and I called Obelix, who was looking everywhere for a roast boar.

'Come on, Obelix. We're off!'

The Roman seemed surprised.

'But legionaries aren't allowed to leave camp!'

'We're not legionaries any more. Come on, let's go!'

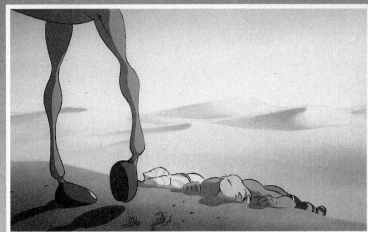

 We made slow progress across the vast expanse of the desert, and we wouldn't have got far if we hadn't spotted . . .

'A caravan! Look, Asterix!'

Sure enough, a long line of Bedouins in sand-coloured robes was riding our way. The leader came to meet us.

'This desert is getting overcrowded,' he remarked. 'Where are you two from?'

'Gaul.'

'You too, you two?'

'What do you mean, you too?'

'We've just sold . . . er, been escorting a couple of Gauls we found in the desert. A man and a woman.'

Sold! So these desert Bedouins were slave merchants! Time they got their just deserts! Wasting no more time on Eastern courtesies, Obelix sent them all flying, slave merchants and camels too. They really had the hump! Then he had an idea, caught two camels by the tail, retrieved them for our own personal use, and we were off.

Practical as ever, Obelix inquired, 'Where are we going now we're not Romans any more, Asterix?'

'To Rome.'

'Rome?'

'Yes, that must be where our friends are to be sold as slaves. And you mark my words – if the Romans give us any trouble, we'll leave their city full of ruins!'

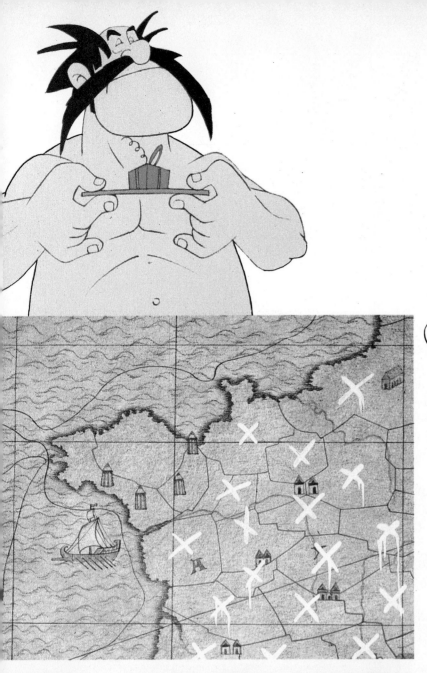

Remember me, Caius Flabius Obtus? It was about time I called on Caesar to tell him the plans I'd made for his triumph. He was sure to be in a good mood today, because slaves from all the countries he had conquered were streaming into Rome, laden with presents.

'O immortal Emperor,' I said, 'your triumph will be a real triumph!'

'I want it to be a celebration worthy of my military renown, Flabius Obtus! A really splendid event!'

'The best ever, O Caesar!'

'So what sort of show are you laying on, Flabius Obtus?'

'Oh, a great show, Caesar! First we release ten thousand doves, then you give the starter's signal for the chariot race. Then it'll be the gladiators. I've got hold of some really magnificent specimens, O Caesar, enormously strong. And then ...'

"Good show!" said Caesar. "It had better be! Succeed, and you'll be the richest man in Rome. Fail, and you'll be part of the show yourself ... in the arena, with the lions!'

Oh help! I saw a hitch coming up. Caesar was going over to the map where a legionary was crossing off the provinces which had sent presents. Any moment now Caesar would spot the fact that ...

'You said presents were coming in from all our provinces?'

'That's right, Caesar! Thousands of presents!'

'From *all* our provinces?'

'Er ... yes, all our provinces ... well, er ...'

'From everywhere? Including a certain little Gaulish village?'

'Er, well, Caesar, everywhere ... or thereabouts ...'

I had to make up for this blunder somehow. I thought I'd better provide plenty of slaves for the Games. Luckily, that day was a common slave-market day of the EEC organization (European Employers of Captives). And there was my old friend Suspicius, who specialized in African imports. How odd . . . it looked as if he had Gauls in stock today.

'Hey, don't you usually sell slaves from Africa, Suspicius?'

'They *are* from Africa, Obtus. They just come from Gaul in the first place.'

'I'm not interested in the girl, but that young man looks good and strong. How much?'

'I'm selling them as a pair. Three thousand sestertii.'

'Three thousand! That's a bit steep!'

'They're very rare! They come from the farthest reaches of Gaul – from Armorica.'

Armorica, I thought. Well, well, well! Indomitable Gauls, I wouldn't be surprised! They'd be a nice surprise for Caesar, and I'd be in his good tablets again. Yes, I MUST HAVE THOSE SLAVES!

'You know, when I spotted you I thought, that's Suspicius . . . isn't his stall bigger than permitted by market regulations? Suppose the Prefect of Rome got to know . . . you'd be out of business!'

'All right, I'll sell you the slaves for two thousand sestertii, how about that?'

'You do have an import permit for your two Gauls, of course? Just in case the Tribune of the City were to ask for it?'

'Let's say a thousand sestertii, Obtus.'

'And . . . er . . . you did renew your slave merchant's licence?'

'Fifty sestertii, O great Flabius Obtus!'

'Just one other thing . . . your taxes are all in order, are they?'

'O immortal Flabius Obtus, allow me to make you a present of these slaves! I should consider it an honour!'

I'd done the trick! Ho, ho, ho! Now I had two indomitable Gauls, I could take them back to Caesar, my head held high.

'Ave, Caesar!'

'Ave, Obtus. Any more news of my triumph?'

'Well, I'm planning a parade of slaves from all your conquered countries!'

'All of them?'

'All of them, Caesar! Even the indomitable Gauls will bow before you in the Circus arena!'

'Never!'

What? What the Hades did that young Gaulish slave mean, never? How dared he answer Caesar back?

'I am Tragicomix, son of an Armorican chief, and Armoricans never will be slaves!'

'You've got a nerve, young Gaul. But that's not a bad idea . . . yes, I'll reserve you for a fate more worthy of you! Lock him up in a cell alone!'

'No, no! I will never leave Tragicomix! I'd rather die!'

It was the girl giving Caesar. garum* this time. And Caesar, in his generosity, granted her wish!

'Die? If that's the way you want it! Put them both in the dungeons under the Colosseum. They're to be thrown to the lions.'

*Roman sauce

As everyone knows, all roads lead to Rome, even in the desert, so we had no difficulty in reaching the Eternal City.

The best way to find Tragicomix and Panacea, sold as slaves by the desert Bedouins, would be to visit the slave market. I'd heard that some of the slave merchants specialized in African imports, and sure enough, we soon found one.

'I say,' I asked, 'you don't happen to have sold a couple of Gauls, do you? A man and a woman?'

'After information, eh? Information will cost you!'

I saw that my friend Obelix was obviously keen to show the slave merchant a thing or two to his own cost, so I left him to settle accounts. I knew he'd beat the man down! Sure enough, when Obelix had paid him out with a smacker or two, there was a slump, and having had more than he'd bargained for, he was free with his information.

'I sold them to a man called Caius Flabius Obtus. You can't miss him. He always wears a red cloak and he goes to the baths every day.'

We went straight to the baths ourselves. A young attendant met us in the entrance hall. 'You must get undressed, noble lords!' he said.

'Is this one of our friends or not?' asked Obelix, puzzled.

'Yes, Obelix, let's just do as he says!'

We left the changing room and made for the sudatorium, but a man stopped us at the door.

'You can't come in here, little titch!'

'Who are you talking to?' asked the baffled Obelix.

'You keep out of this, fatty!'

'This lot aren't our friends, are they, Asterix?'

'It doesn't look like it!'

'Goody!'

And my large friend sent the man flying.

I realized that we weren't about to find a red cloak with Flabius Obtus inside it in a place where everyone was undressed. So I gave the next order of the bath: retreat in good order.

But Obelix, who had seen a swimming pool, had other ideas. He jumped straight in. However, there wasn't room for two: it was either him or the water. The water left.

Not best pleased, I shoved him towards the changing room, where we found Dogmatix waiting. Obelix wanted to stop and play with his dog. I had to explain that it was Flabius Obtus's footsteps we should be dogging.

However, he wasn't listening. 'Who's been a good little doggie, then?'

This was getting me down! 'Hurry up, you mutt!' I said. '*Both* you mutts! We can't hang about here! Come on, Obelix!'

'Oh, so I'm in the doghouse for petting my dog now, is that it, Mister Asterix?'

'Oh, so I'm being petty now, is that it, Mister Obelix? Come on, we're in a hurry!'

'And you can stop shouting. You'll frighten Dogmatix!'

'I am not shouting, Obelix!'

'I'M NOT SHOUTING EITHER!'

Every minute counted, so I went off on my own, leaving Obelix to finish dressing.

He'd find me all right by himself.

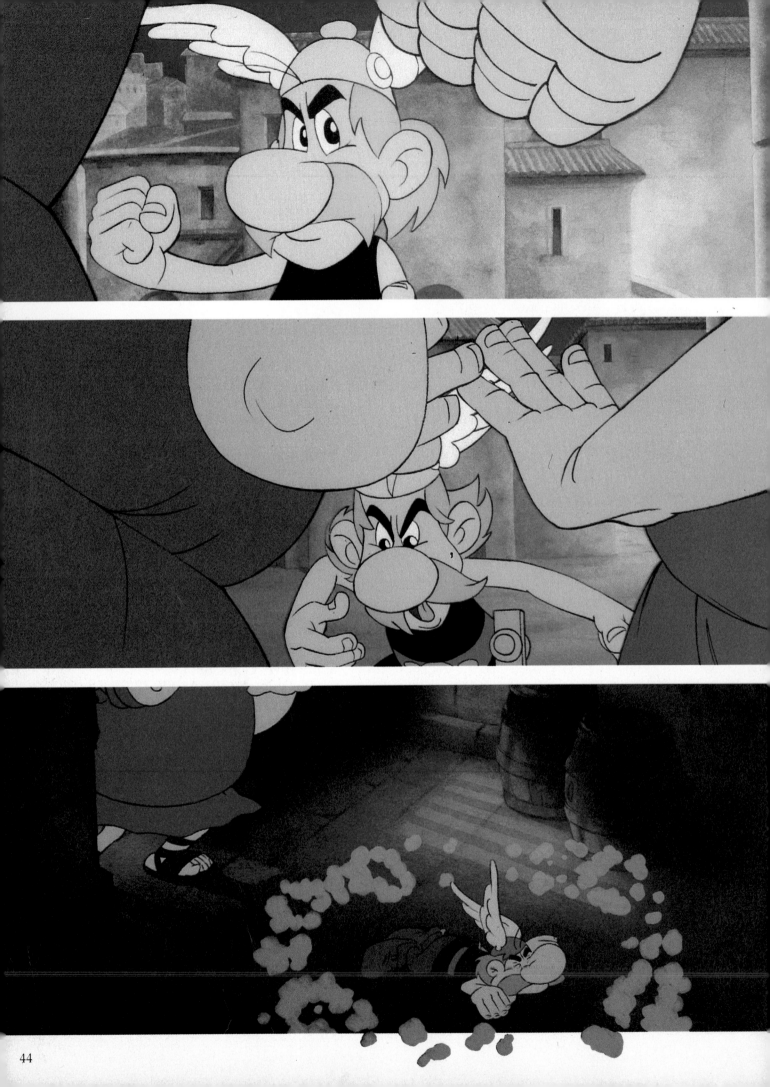

However, the noise we'd been making had roused the neighbourhood. Some men came towards me. "Do you happen to know Caius Flabius Obtus?' I asked.

'You bet! Ho, ho! He's Caesar's head gladiator-trainer, and he takes a great interest in you! Get him!' the man told his friends.

Quick – now for a slug of magic potion . . . but where was my gourd? By Belisama, I'd lost it! I was done for! Help! Where was Obelix?

I was cast into a dungeon, all alone. There was a tremendous storm raging outside. I could hear thunder. What was Obelix doing? Where was he? Come to think of it, why was I here anyway? *Why* did Flabius Obtus take a great interest in me? Perhaps he'd seen us at the baths and been impressed by Obelix's muscle, and he thought I was Obelix's trainer . . . and then again, where *was* Obelix? He must be looking for me! I imagined him wandering the streets of Rome, shouting my name.

And to think I'd gone and lost my gourd . . . where was it? Who'd taken it? Oh, if only Dogmatix was here! He'd soon find it for me!

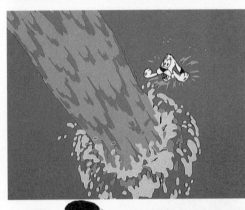

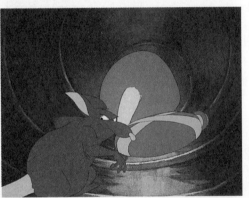

If my own indomitable reputation was under a cloud, so was Rome – under a cloudburst, in fact. The rain running down the Roman roads ran down into my cell too.

Where *could* Obelix be? The water was still rising. I was up to my neck in it now! I'd be drowned ... oh, help! 'Obelix!' I shouted. 'Help! I'm here! Help!'

'Asterix! Asterix!!!'

Obelix at last! I heard him calling! He was looking for me, but he couldn't see me! Then he spotted my helmet, floating on the water. He was coming! He wrenched the bars of the cell away, plunged into the water, and helped me out.

'Asterix!'

'Obelix!' I said. 'About time too!'

We were reunited, friends again!

'The trouble is, I've lost my magic potion.'

'And I've lost my little dog ... I wonder where he is?'

The storm was over. The Colosseum was bathed in moonlight. In the silence, we heard a woman singing. People were stopping to listen, moved to tears. A passing Roman explained.

'She's a Gaulish prisoner. She sings like that every night.'

'Gaulish, did you say?'

'That's right. She's to be thrown to the lions on the day of Caesar's triumph.'

PANACEA!

By Toutatis, we couldn't have this! I was furious! 'If only I had my gourd!' I said crossly, out loud.

'What was that?'

'Oh . . . er . . . I just said the circus is well gourded. I mean guarded.'

'You bet! Nobody gets in there except condemned prisoners, lions and gladiators!'

Panacea's song still echoed through the Roman night. I drew Obelix aside.

'Listen – we're going to be in there ourselves on the day of Caesar's triumph. We're about to become gladiators!'

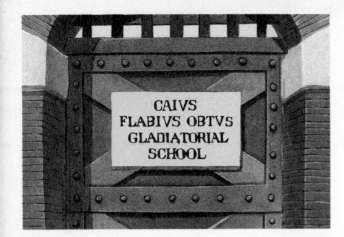

No sooner said than done. First thing next morning, we rolled up to the doors of the gladiatorial school. We saw a man waving his arms about and shouting – Flabius Obtus, very likely.

'I must have those two men!' he was yelling. 'Both of them, the fat one and the little one. I want the whole staff combing the city for them. And I want them here today! Understand? Get it?'

I interrupted these melodious remarks.

'Are you Caius Flabius Obtus?'

'Am I ... what ... oo-er ... I d-d-don't ...'

'We want to see Caius Flabius Obtus.'

'Yes, I mean no, er ... listen, I can explain everything, it's quite simple really, I ...'

'We want to be gladiators.'

He seemed to relax all of a sudden!

'Gladiators? You *want* to be gladiators? In that case, yes, I *am* Caius Flabius Obtus!'

In fact, he was relaxing a bit too much.

'So you want to be gladiators? Ho, ho, ho! I shall put you in the hands of the most terrible of my trainers, the savage Dubius Status!'

Well, well, well! If it wasn't our old friend Dubius Status! He didn't seem too pleased to see us.

'No! No! Mercy!' he babbled. 'Mercy! I can't bear it! Anything but that! I never want to set eyes on those two again.'

'We want to be gladiators, Dubius Status. Come on, teach us how, do!'

Pulling himself together, Dubius Status took us to an arena where our future companions were training, and introduced us.

'A couple of new recruits, gladiators! Train them for me, will you?'

50

And off he went, slamming the door behind him! Our new friends didn't look particularly welcoming ... but we'd learned to defend ourselves the hard way in the Foreign Legion, as the gladiators soon discovered to their cost.

Seeing us emerge from the arena unharmed, Dubius Status began quivering all over, like a wild boar the day before a Gaulish victory, and chased off to give notice.

'I'm packing it in, Flabius Obtus!'

'And where are you going?'

'First to apply for my veteran's pension, then back to making lace in my father's lace factory!'

The great day had come! By Juno, these would be magnificent Games!

An eager, sensation-seeking crowd filled the seats of the Colosseum. Suddenly trumpets sounded, announcing Caesar's arrival in the Imperial Box. Tantantaraa! It was music to the Emperor's ears. Sidling up to the great man, I murmured into those same Imperial ears, 'Yes, your triumph will be a real triumph, O Caesar! Rome's never seen anything like it! You're in for a surprise. This is going to be an amazing show!'

'I hope so, Flabius Obtus, because if not, you'll be in on the act. Let the games begin!'

And the white doves were released to mark the start of Caesar's triumph.

The announcer, or stentor, announced the first item on the programme.

'And now for the long-awaited moment of ... THE CHARIOT RACE!'

Everything was all right so far ... it didn't look as if I was about to end my career inside a lion ... Here came the first chariot. Oh no! Oh, by Minerva! What were those two Gauls doing here? They were supposed to come on with the gladiators, not the charioteers! Oh dear, oh dear, oh dear ... Caesar didn't look as if he thought much of this at all.

'Two men on a two-wheeler? I don't care for these flights of fancy, Caius Flabius Obtus!'

If only they'd tried to look inconspicuous, but not them, oh no! Those two clowns had to make a performance of everything. What a circus!

If I knew them, they'd manage to come in first!

There! I knew it!

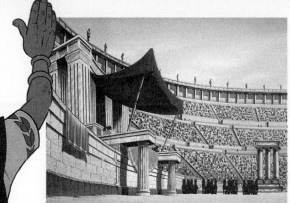
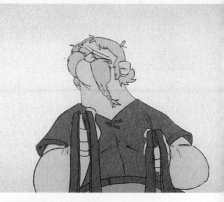

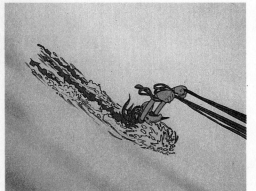

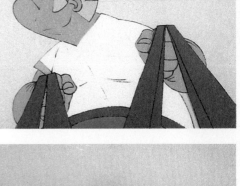

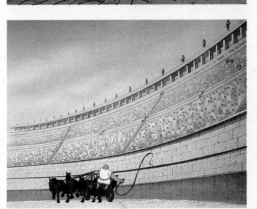

Phew! The stentor was announcing the next item. What a relief! 'And now for the star turn: we present the gladiators. Specially trained by Caius Flabius Obtus to make Caesar's triumph the greatest show business triumph ever!'

'I'm rather pleased with this one, Caesar,' I explained. 'You just wait . . . there are a couple of amazing performers among those men!'

'Ave Caesar, we who are about to die salute you,' said most of the gladiators.

'Hi, Julius, old boy!' said two of the gladiators. 'How's tricks?'

Those Gauls again!

'Er . . . they're not very well educated, Caesar . . . but they're terrific gladiators! Real fighting machines! The crowd will love it!'

I never spoke a truer word . . . the Gauls were chatting casually to each other as they knocked out all my gladiators one by one!

'I say, Asterix, are this lot friends of ours?'

'Not so far as I know, Obelix.'

'I get a bit muddled, you see. They were our enemies in Gaul and our friends in Africa. Maybe good old Julius can explain.'

Good old Julius was not looking a bit pleased. I needed the lions, and fast! The lions couldn't fail me! Caesar was sure to like the lions!

'They're ravenous, O Caesar! All they've had since we captured them is a yoghourt a day!'

The stentor informed the crowd that two Gauls, Tragicomix and Panacea (not Asterix and Obelix for once, thank Jupiter!) were about to be thrown to the lions, and the Emperor would magnanimously allow them to defend themselves with their bare hands!

At this moment, the following remarks were heard in the arena:
'My dog!'
'My magic potion!'

And sure enough, a small dog came chasing in, ahead of the most ferocious lions in the entire empire. 'My little Dogmatix!' cried the big fat Gaul (oh no, not him again!). The other Gaul, the little one, seized the gourd the dog was holding in its mouth. It seemed to be a touching family reunion ...

Was I dreaming, or what? Where did those two think they were? Ah, good! At long last the fat one was taking an interest!

'Lions! Lions! Goody, goody, goody!'

They were crazy! They must be crazy! There they were in front of a hundred thousand spectators, including Julius Caesar himself. About to be eaten alive by lions. And what were they doing? Laughing their heads off!

A gourd sailed through the air. The slave Tragicomix caught it and drank from it. Incredible! Stopping for a drink, just as if he'd popped into the local taverna!

Luckily the lions were racing in ... they'd soon get things back to normal!

Oh no! They didn't! The Gaul who had been drinking sent the wild beasts sailing through the air and into the audience. There was panic as the spectators fled, howling with terror ...

And to cap it all, Obelix, the fat one, collided with a marble column as he saw the pretty Gaulish girl Panacea pass by. The marble column crashed to the ground. Everything around us started to shake.

'You were right, Obtus,' commented Caesar, stony-faced. 'An amazing show. A great surprise! Rome has never seen anything like it.'

And before I could say a word, the four Gauls had marched up to him.

'Be generous, O Caesar!' begged Asterix. 'Show mercy to these two courageous slaves!'

'The magnanimity of Caesar knows no bounds,' said the great man. 'Well, *almost* no bounds . . .'

His icy glare chilled me to the bone.

'However, you four are free!' he told the Gauls.

When we got home, our friends in the village gave *us* a lovely surprise, just the same as usual. A magnificent banquet! Chief Vital-statistix called for silence and climbed on the table to make a speech.

'Friends, Gauls, countrymen! Caesar's triumph ended in a famous Gaulish victory! It is to the Emperor whose blah-blah-blah . . . courageous blah-blah-blah . . . extraordinary blah-blah-blah . . . that we owe blah-blah-blah . . . vote of thanks . . . I wish to lay a proposal on the table . . .'

But amidst this rolling oratory the chief rolled over a barrel and was laid on the table himself, right in the middle of the sausages.

Meanwhile Tragicomix and Panacea were thanking us. Tragicomix said Obelix had been marvellous. And guess what? Panacea gave me a kiss, which . . . honestly, how childish can you get? . . . well, the fact is, it brought a blush to my cheeks, I can't deny that it really made me feel most odd, I came over all peculiar . . . yes, it gave me a kind of vague, happy feeling, that's what it did, and taking no more notice of the others, I went off alone to dream my dreams . . .

THE END